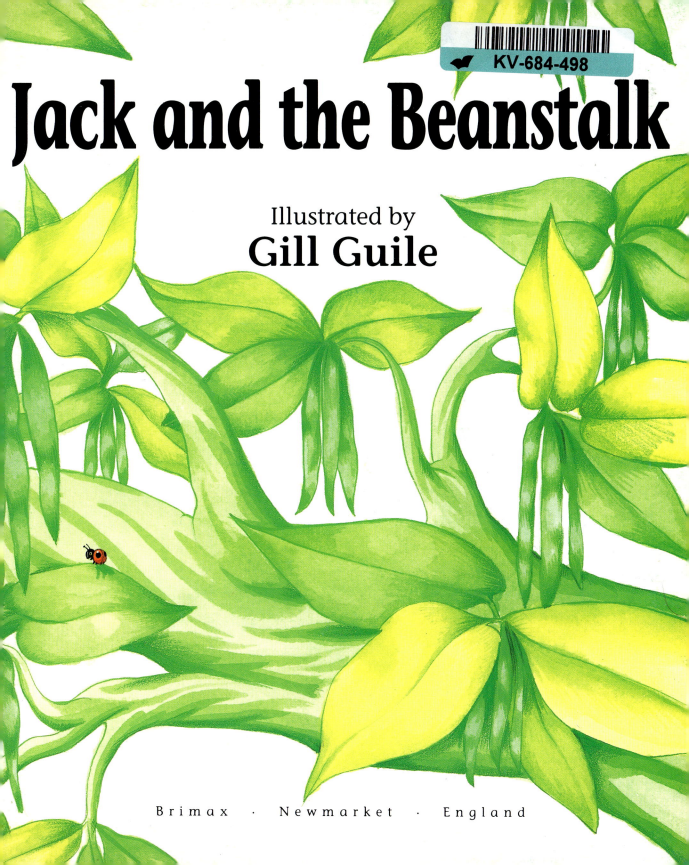

Jack and the Beanstalk

Illustrated by
Gill Guile

Brimax · Newmarket · England

Jack and his mother are very poor. Jack decides to go to market to sell their cow. On the way he meets a man who says, "Is your cow for sale?" "Yes, she is," says Jack. "I will give you five magic beans for her," says the man. Jack takes the beans and hurries home.

Jack's mother is very angry when she hears what Jack has done. She throws the beans out of the window and sends Jack to bed without any supper. When Jack wakes up the next day, there is an enormous beanstalk outside his bedroom window.

Jack decides to climb up the beanstalk. He climbs higher and higher until he finds himself in another world above the clouds. He walks along a path until he comes to a huge house. He knocks as hard as he can on the door. It is opened by a giant's wife. She invites Jack in and gives him some breakfast.

While Jack is still eating he hears heavy footsteps and a loud voice shouting, "Fee-fi-fo-fum, I smell the blood of an Englishman!"
"That is my husband," says the woman. "You must hide in the oven. He likes to eat boys like you for breakfast."

The giant is sure he can smell a boy, but he cannot find Jack. After his breakfast, the giant asks for his magic hen. Jack peeks out of the oven. The giant says, "Lay, hen!" and the hen lays a golden egg.

"Mother would like to own a hen like that," whispers Jack.

Jack waits until the giant is asleep. He picks up the hen and tucks it inside his shirt. He sneaks from the house, runs along the path and climbs down the beanstalk. He gives the magic hen to his mother. She is very pleased to see Jack.

The next morning, Jack climbs up the beanstalk again. He slips under the giant's door and hides in the kitchen drawer. "Fee-fi-fo-fum, I smell the blood of an Englishman!" roars the giant. He looks for Jack but cannot find him. Then the giant calls for his golden harp and says, "Play, harp!" The harp plays without the giant touching the strings.

When the giant falls asleep, Jack creeps out of the drawer. As he picks up the harp it calls, "Master! Wake up!" The giant roars with anger at Jack. He chases him out of the house and along the path until they reach the beanstalk. Jack climbs down as fast as he can. His mother hands him an axe. With one mighty blow, Jack cuts through the beanstalk.

The beanstalk and the giant crash to the ground. They make a hole so deep they are never seen again. Jack and his mother live happily ever after.

Now that they have the magic hen that lays golden eggs and the harp that sings by itself, they will never be poor again.

Can you find five differences between these two pictures?